For Olivia.

——*MW*

Published by
PEACHTREE PUBLISHERS
1700 Chattahoochee Avenue
Atlanta, Georgia 30318

www.peachtree-online.com

First published by ABC Books for
the Australian Broadcasting Corporation in 2000.

First United States edition published by
Peachtree Publishers in 2001.

10 9 8 7 6 5 4 3 2

Cataloging-in-Publication data for this book
is available from the Library of Congress.

The illustrations were painted with watercolor.
Type font: Venetian
Designed and typeset by Monkeyfish
Color separations by Modern Age, Hong Kong
Printed in Singapore by Tien Wah Press

Nighty Night!

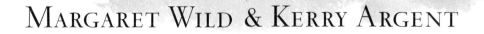

MARGARET WILD & KERRY ARGENT

Ω

PEACHTREE
ATLANTA

One evening as the sun was going down, the baby animals played and played and wouldn't stop playing. So Mother Sheep, Father Duck, Mother Hen, and Father Pig called, "Come on, everyone—off to your beds now, little ones!"

"Nighty night, my lovely lambs,"
said Mother Sheep, as she went
to tuck her little ones in.

"Cheep! Cheep! Tricked you!"
said the chicks.

"You little rascals!
You're not my
lovely lambs!"
said Mother Sheep.

"Sweet dreams, my darling ducklings,"
said Father Duck, as he went
to tuck his little ones in.

"Oink! Oink! Surprise!"
said the piglets.

"You sassy scalawags!
You're not my darling ducklings!"
said Father Duck.

"Good night, my chicky chicks," said Mother Hen, as she went to tuck her little ones in.

"Baa! Baa! Boo!" said the lamb.
"You naughty scamps!
You're not my chicky chicks!"
said Mother Hen.

"Sleep tight, my precious piglets,"
said Father Pig, as he went
to tuck his little ones in.

"Quack! Quack! Fooled you!"
said the ducklings.

"You fluffy tricksters!
You're not my
precious piglets!"
said Father Pig.

"You little rascals!"

"You sassy scalawags!"

"You naughty scamps!"

"You fluffy tricksters!"

"Off to your beds now, everyone!"

"Nighty night, my lovely lambs,"

said Mother Sheep with a loving baa baa.

"Not yet!" said the lambs.
"Tell us one more story, please!"

"Sweet dreams, my darling ducklings,"

said Father Duck with a fond quack quack.

"Not yet!" said the ducklings.
"We want ten kisses each!"

"Good night, my chicky chicks,"

said Mother Hen with a gentle cluck cluck.

"Not yet!" said the chicks. "We're thirsty!"

"Sleep tight, my precious piglets,"

said Father Pig with a tender oink oink.

"Not yet!" said the piglets.
"We have to wee,

wee,

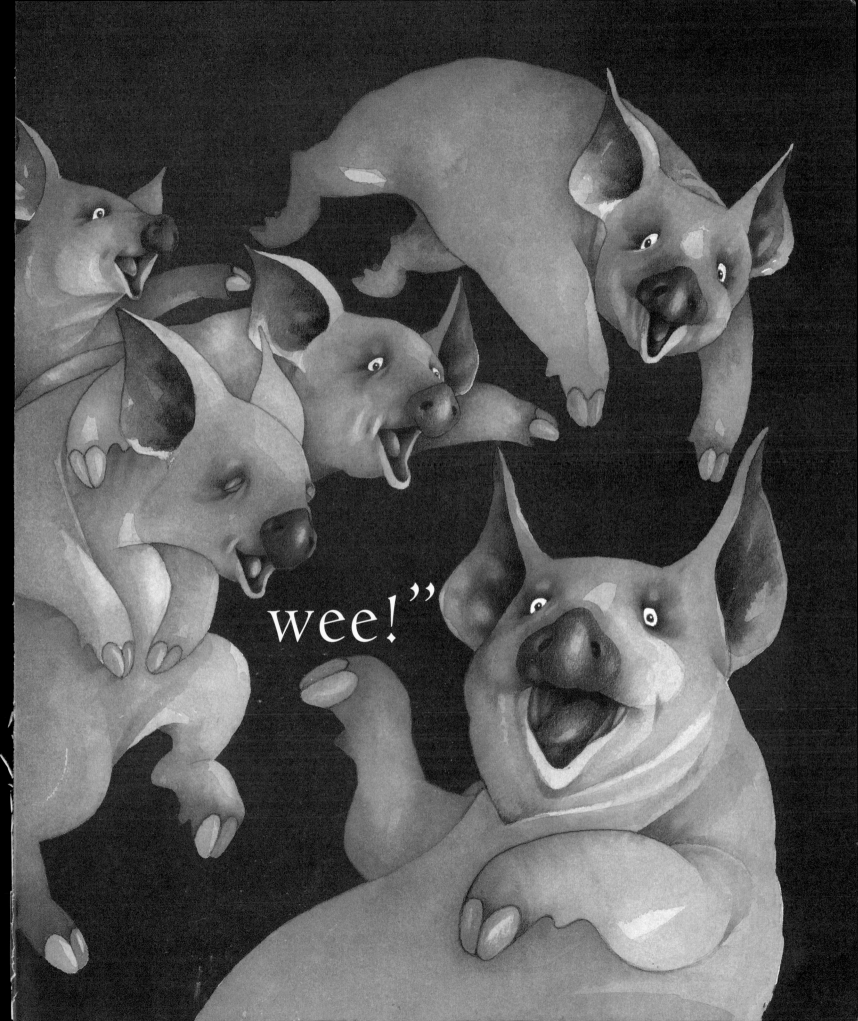

"No more tricks now."

"Settle down."

"Snuggle up."

"Sleep tight."

"Nighty night!"